Mr. Bear's New Baby

DEBI GLIORI

ORCHARD BOOKS
New York

This book is dedicated
to families everywhere for whom
an uninterrupted night's sleep
is just a distant memory.

Copyright © 1999 by Debi Gliori
First American edition 1999 published by Orchard Books
First published in Great Britain in 1999 by Orchard Books London
Debi Gliori asserts the moral right to be identified as the author/illustrator of this work.

Orchard Books, A Grolier Company, 95 Madison Avenue, New York, NY 10016

Manufactured in Belgium
Book design by Helene Wald Berinsky
The text of this book is set in 16 point Veljovic Medium.

1 3 5 7 9 10 8 6 4 2

Library of Congress Cataloging-in-Publication Data
Gliori, Debi.
Mr. Bear's new baby / Debi Gliori. — 1st American ed.
p. cm.
Summary: Mr. and Mrs. Bear and the other forest animals despair of
ever getting Baby Bear to stop crying and go to sleep, but Small Bear
knows just how to solve the problem.
ISBN 0-531-30152-4 (alk. paper)
[1. Bears—Fiction. 2. Babies—Fiction. 3. Crying—Fiction.
4. Family life—Fiction.] I. Title.
PZ7.G4889Mr 1999
[E]—dc21   98–30530

It is way past bedtime in the forest.
It is time for everyone to be asleep.
A dark and quiet time for hush and lullabies.

But lights are on at Mr. Bear's house.
And listen . . . drifting out over the trees
is the most awful din.
It's the sound of Mr. Bear's new baby
crying.

"Oh dear," sighed Mrs. Bear.
"Oh dear, oh dear," groaned Mr. Bear.
"Waaaa," cried the new baby.

"What that baby needs is to be tucked in by her daddy," said Mr. Bear.

He climbed out of bed and went to tuck in the new baby.

But the baby cried more loudly.
Mr. Bear gazed lovingly at the baby.

"What that baby needs is some milk from her mommy," said Mr. Bear.

And Mrs. Bear climbed out of bed and fed the new baby.

But the new baby spluttered and choked and cried some more.

Mr. Bear paced up and down, patting the new baby's back. But the new baby closed her eyes, threw back her head, and let out a huge wail.

"Goodness," said Mr. Bear. "What an enormous mouth for one so small. What you need is a lullaby." Mr. and Mrs. Bear sang the new baby a lullaby. But that didn't work either.

There was a knock at the door.
In staggered Mr. Bun with a rocking cradle.

"Try this," he said, yawning. "When our six babies were small, this used to put them to sleep."

So Mr. Bear tucked his new baby into the cradle, and they all took turns rocking her.

But the cradle was too wobbly, and the new baby still cried.

There was another knock on the door.
In came Mrs. Hoot-Toowit with a huge nest.
"I don't know if this will work for new
baby bears," she said. "But when
Little Howl was a baby, I would put her
in it, and she would fall asleep at once."

So Mr. Bear lifted the new baby out of
the rocking cradle and put her in the nest.
But the nest was too prickly, and the new
baby continued to cry.

"Heavens," said Mr. Bear, feeling
pretty close to crying himself,
"how can someone so small
make so much noise?"

One by one, all of Mr. Bear's sleepless neighbors
came calling with things to help the new baby sleep.

Mr. Rivet-Frog brought
his children's favorite lily pad.
But that was too wet.

Mrs. Buzz brought her infant's hive.
But that was too sticky.

Even Mrs. Grizzle-Bear brought
Baby Grizzle-Bear's shawl.
But that was too woolly.

While Mrs. Grizzle-Bear poured tea and Mrs. Bear passed cake around, Mr. Bear paced up and down with the sobbing baby over his shoulder.

"Little one," he said. "My legs are tired from all this walking."

But the baby kept on crying.

Mr. Bear patted the baby gently on her back
and whispered in her ear. "Baby bear," he said.
"My shoulder is soggy from all these tears."
The baby cried all the more.
"Good grief," said Mr. Bear, feeling tired,
soggy, and very fed up. "What on earth
can I do to stop you from crying?"

A little figure appeared at the door, trailing a blanket behind her.

"Whatever are you doing up?" said Mrs. Bear.

"I can't sleep," said Small Bear. "That baby woke me."

"You're too small to be up this late," groaned Mrs. Bear. "Come on, back to bed."

"She's even smaller than I am," said Small Bear. "And she's up."

The new baby looked at her with a woebegone little hiccup.

"I'm much bigger than both of you," sighed Mr. Bear, "and all I want is not to be up."

"We'd better be going home to bed," said Mr. Bun and Mrs. Hoot-Toowit.

"Good-night all," croaked Mr. Rivet-Frog.

"Sleep well," added Mrs. Buzz.

"I'll come back for the shawl in the morning," said Mrs. Grizzle-Bear.

All of Mr. Bear's neighbors tiptoed out, leaving Mr. and Mrs. Bear with their wakeful little bears. The new baby was still crying.

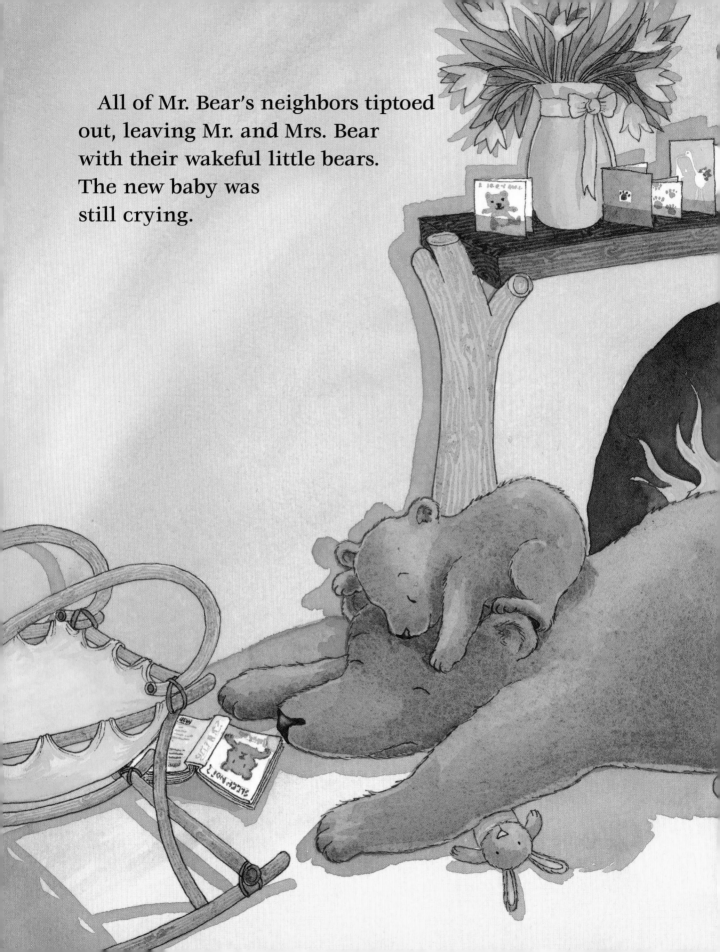

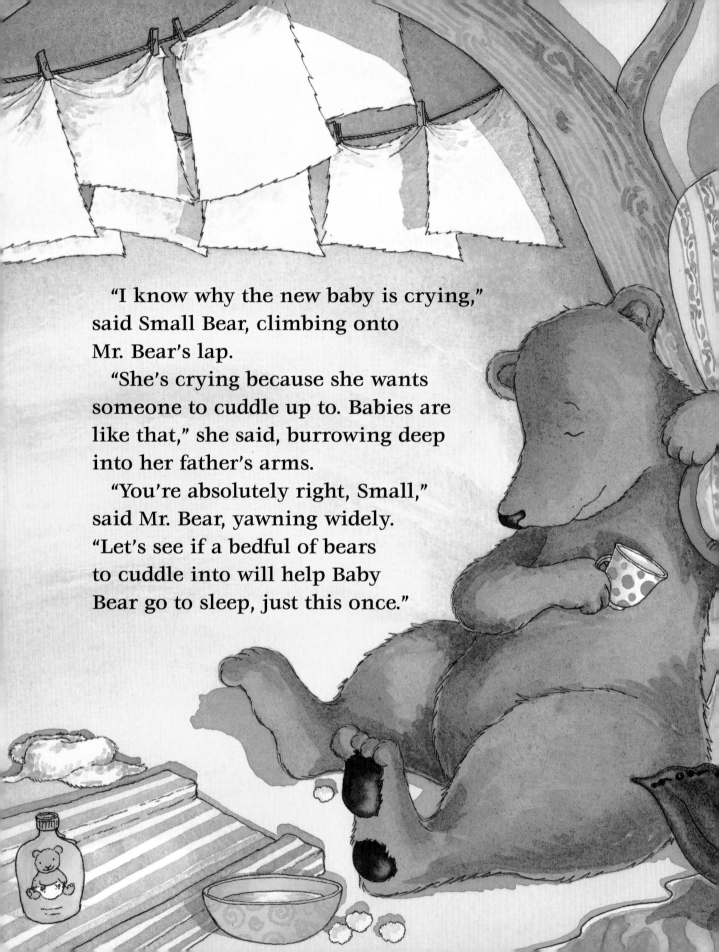

"I know why the new baby is crying," said Small Bear, climbing onto Mr. Bear's lap.

"She's crying because she wants someone to cuddle up to. Babies are like that," she said, burrowing deep into her father's arms.

"You're absolutely right, Small," said Mr. Bear, yawning widely. "Let's see if a bedful of bears to cuddle into will help Baby Bear go to sleep, just this once."

Carrying their little bears,
Mr. and Mrs. Bear climbed
upstairs to bed.

Mr. and Mrs. Bear's bed wasn't wobbly or prickly.
Nor was it wet, sticky, or woolly.
In fact it was utter bliss....
The new baby stopped crying immediately,
gazed into Mr. Bear's eyes, patted his nose, and
fell fast asleep.

"My goodness," said Mr. Bear, stunned by the
sudden silence.

"Well done, Small," said Mrs. Bear, turning over
and starting to snore almost at once.

But Small Bear was fast asleep and dreaming
of being big, and very soon, all was quiet and still.

The house was full of the sound of sleeping bears.
All, that is, except for Mr. Bear.

He lay in the dark, listening to Mrs. Bear
snoring and, far off in the trees,
the sound of Mrs. Hoot-Toowit
singing lullabies.
The baby stretched like a
furry starfish and smiled
in her sleep.
"How can someone so
small take up so much
room?" wondered Mr. Bear.

The last thing he heard before he
fell asleep was Mrs. Hoot-Toowit's
"Good-night, good-night to you, to you."